Feathered Friends

Cover illustration by JON GOODELL

Illustrations by
LISA BERRETT
KRISTA BRAUCKMANN-TOWNS
JANE CHAMBLESS WRIGHT
DREW-BROOK-CORMACK ASSOCIATES
KATE STURMAN GORMAN
JUDITH DUFOUR LOVE
BEN MAHAN
ANASTASIA MITCHELL
ANITA NELSON
ROSARIO VALDERRAMA

Louis Weber, C.E.O.
Publications International, Ltd.
7373 North Cicero Avenue
Lincolnwood, Illinois 60646

PUBLICATIONS INTERNATIONAL, LTD.

Rainbow Books is a trademark of Publications International, Ltd.

Answer to a Child's Question

Do you ask what the birds say? The sparrow, the dove,
    The linnet and thrush say, "I love and I love!"
In the winter they are silent—the wind is so strong;
    What it says, I don't know, but it sings a loud song.
But green leaves, and blossoms, and sunny warm weather,
    And singing, and loving—all come back together.
But the lark is so brimful of gladness and love,
    The green fields below him, the blue sky above,
That he sings, and he sings and forever sings he:
    "I love my love, and my love loves me."

The Canary

Mary had a little bird,
    With feathers bright and yellow,
Slender legs—upon my word,
    He was a pretty fellow.

Sweetest notes he always sung,
    Which much delighted Mary;
Often when his cage was hung,
    She sat to hear Canary.

The Owl in the Tree

There was an owl lived in an oak,
  Whiskey, whaskey, wheedle;
The only words he ever spoke
  Were fiddle, faddle, feedle.

An old man chanced to come that way,
  Whiskey, whaskey, wheedle;
Says he, "I see you, silly bird,
  So fiddle, faddle, feedle."

The Owl and the Pussycat

The owl and the pussycat went to sea
   In a beautiful pea-green boat.
They took some honey, and plenty of money,
   Wrapped up in a five-pound note.
The owl looked up to the stars above,
   And sang to a small guitar,
"O lovely Pussy! O Pussy, my love,
   What a beautiful Pussy you are,
You are, you are!
   What a beautiful Pussy you are!"

The Duck

Behold the duck.
　　It does not cluck.
A cluck it lacks.
　　It quacks.
'Tis especially fond
　　Of a puddle or pond.
When it dines or sups,
　　It bottoms up.

The Robin

When up aloft
   I fly and fly
I see in pools
   The shining sky,
And a happy bird
   Am I, am I!

The Moon

The moon has a face like a clock in the hall;
   She shines on thieves on the garden wall,
On streets and fields and harbor quays,
   And birdies asleep in the forks of the trees.

The squalling cat and the squeaking mouse,
   The howling dog by the door of the house,
The bat that lies in bed at noon,
   All love to be out by the light of the moon.

The Owl

When cats run home and light is come,
    And dew is cold upon the ground,
And the far-off stream is dumb,
    And the whirring sail goes round,
And the whirring sail goes round;
    Alone and warming his five wits,
The white owl in the belfry sits.

When merry milkmaids click the latch,
    And sweetly smells the new-mown hay,
And the rooster sings beneath the thatch,
    Twice or thrice his roundelay,
Twice or thrice his roundelay;
    Alone and warming his five wits,
The white owl in the belfry sits.

The Brown Thrush

There's a merry brown thrush sitting up in the tree.
　　She's singing to me! She's singing to me!
And what does she say, little girl, little boy?
　　"Oh the world's running over with joy!
Don't you hear? Don't you see?
　　Hush! Look! In my tree,
I'm as happy as happy can be!"

Time to Rise

A birdie with a yellow bill
    Hopped upon the window sill,
Tipped his shining eye, and said:
    "Aren't you ashamed, you sleepy-head?"

The North Wind Doth Blow

The north wind doth blow,
   And we shall have snow,
And what will the robin do then, poor thing?
   He'll sit in a barn,
And keep himself warm,
   And hide his head under his wing, poor thing.

The north wind doth blow,
   And we shall have snow,
And what will the children do then, poor things?
   When lessons are done,
They must skip, jump, and run,
   Until they have made themselves warm, poor things.

Bedtime

The evening is coming,
   The sun sinks to rest;
The rooks are all flying
   Straight home to the nest.
"Caw!" says the rook, as he flies overhead,
   "It's time little people were going to bed!"